A CHRIS

S. A. Carmody

A Christmas Carol Rewired

First published in Great Britain in 2025 by
KMCS Publishing
www.kmcspublishing.com
Paperback ISBN: 9781918259018
eBook ISBN: 9781918259025
Cover design: KMCS Publishing
The moral right of the author has been asserted.
Publisher's typographical arrangement © 2025 KMCS Publishing.
Printed in UK
10 9 8 7 6 5 4 3 2 1

Contents

Preface

Why retell a story that has already stood the test of nearly two centuries? Dickens's A Christmas Carol has never truly faded from public memory. It has been staged, filmed, parodied, and quoted so often that even those who have never read it can still recognise the ghosts, the miser, and the message of redemption at its heart.

And yet, familiarity can sometimes dull the edge of a story. We think we know Scrooge so well that we stop listening to him. The London he haunted feels sepia-toned, long gone, and easy to dismiss as "the old world." But Dickens did not write for nostalgia. He wrote for urgency. His London was full of poverty and excess, cruelty and kindness, indifference and hope. His tale was not just about Christmas cheer but about what happens when wealth blinds us to humanity.

That urgency still belongs to us. Our cities may be filled with skyscrapers and stock exchanges rather than workhouses and counting houses, but the gap between rich and poor, the question of how we treat the vulnerable, and the temptation to measure life only in profit remain just as sharp. For that reason, I wanted to bring Dickens's story into the present: to place its ghosts in modern streets, its shadows in glass towers, and its redemption in the heart of a man whose wealth has left him poor in spirit.

This is not a replacement for Dickens's tale, nothing could be. Instead, it is an invitation to hear it afresh. The characters you meet may wear new names and live in our time, but their struggles are the same, and their choices just as vital.

If, by the end of this book, you see a little
more of yourself in Edward Sloane, or feel
a tug of hope in his transformation, then
Dickens's message has found its way once
again into the present day. That, I believe
is the true spirit of A Christmas Carol: not
to be preserved in amber, but to be retold
renewed, and lived.

— S. A. Carmody

CHAPTER ONE:

MARLEY'S GHOST

Edward Sloane did not believe in wasting time, money, or kindness. Of the three, he thought kindness the most extravagant. It gave no return, generated no revenue, and could not be entered neatly into a spreadsheet. Numbers were his true companions, and numbers had never betrayed him, unlike people, unlike partners, unlike the world itself.

On Christmas Eve, as the lights of London blinked red and gold across the

Thames, Sloane sat in his glass-walled office twenty-six floors above the City. The skyline glittered: towers glowing like circuit boards, cranes with warning beacons blinking into the night like WhatsApp notifications demanding attention. His multiple monitors displayed real-time market data from Tokyo, New York, Frankfurt, a global web of profit that never slept. To the people on the pavements far below, huddled around their phone screens taking selfies with Christmas lights, the city might have looked magical, festive even. To Sloane, it was simply the marketplace, awake, restless, waiting to be exploited.

The heating in the office was set deliberately low. Climate control was expensive, and comfort was a weakness. His staff wore coats indoors, fingers stiff as they tapped at laptops running outdated software he refused to upgrade. They clutched reusable coffee cups like talismans, the company's pathetic nod to sustainability while Sloane's private jet burned through fuel on monthly trips to Dubai. It kept them sharp; he told himself. Comfort dulled discipline. He sat with his jacket folded over the back of his chair, shirtsleeves rolled to his elbows, Apple Watch tracking his elevated heart rate, eyes flicking between two phones laid on the desk like duelling pistols.

Across the room, Ben Carter hunched over a spreadsheet so bloated it would crash Excel on any five-year-old office PC. Mid-thirties, cheap tie creased from a Primark two-for-one deal, eyes heavy with lack of sleep. He scrolled through endless rows of data, the blue light casting shadows under his eyes. He had three children at home and a wife waiting with mince pies from Tesco and tinsel from Poundland, but none of that mattered to Sloane. "Finish the projections before you leave," Sloane had told him, knowing full well Ben would miss his children's bedtime stories again. It was already nearly seven, and the Uber surge pricing would be astronomical.

The double doors slid open with a hush of expensive engineering. In bounced Freddie Sloane, nephew and nuisance. He was in his twenties, all vintage thrift shop scarf and artfully messy hair, the sort of man who quoted films on Instagram stories and never seemed to own a proper suit. His phone case was covered in stickers from bands Edward had never heard of, and he carried a paper bag that smelled of expensive chocolate, the kind you bought from Borough Market rather than the corner shop.

"Merry Christmas, Ed!" he said, dropping the bag on the desk between a Bloomberg terminal and a stress ball Sloane had never used. "Picked up those truffles you like. The ones from that place in Bermondsey. Thought I'd tempt you into coming over tomorrow. Mum's doing a proper spread, roast goose, bread sauce, the works. She's even got that sourdough starter she's been posting about on Facebook."

Edward Sloane did not glance up from his phone, where notifications from his portfolio management app blinked like Christmas lights. "I don't do Christmas, Freddie. You know that. And I don't eat carbohydrates."

Freddie grinned anyway, pulling out his own phone to snap a picture of his uncle looking particularly Scrooge-like, though he'd never post it, not really. "It's not about the food. It's about being with family. Come on. You spend every holiday in this tower staring at numbers that'll be different tomorrow anyway. One day won't kill your profit margins."

"Family is overrated," Sloane muttered, typing a response to an email from Singapore. "And truffles are a tax dodge. You're wasting your money; money I assume came from that trust fund you pretend not to have."

Ben Carter coughed into his sleeve, pretending to be absorbed in the monitor while actually checking his phone for messages from his wife. The Wi-Fi was deliberately throttled to discourage personal use, but he'd found a way around it. Everyone knew Ben was underpaid, overworked, and somehow grateful for the scraps Sloane tossed him. His

LinkedIn profile still listed "junior analyst" despite five years of senior-level work.

"You're freezing your staff in here, Ed," Freddie said, glancing at Ben with sympathy. "It's December. Even warehouses have heating. Even Scrooge let Bob Cratchit have a fire."

Edward finally looked up, narrowing his eyes. "Who?"

"Never mind." Freddie shook his head, recognising the futility. His uncle hadn't read a book that wasn't about business strategy since university. "Just... think about it, yeah? Christmas dinner. Half past two. I'll keep a seat open. Mum's even making those roast potatoes you used to love."

"Used to" being the operative phrase. Edward had trained himself out of most pleasures years ago.

With that, Freddie was gone, sustainable canvas tote bag swinging, cheer following him out of the building like a YouTube influencer's ring light had briefly illuminated the corporate gloom.

Silence returned, broken only by the clatter of Ben's keyboard and the persistent ping of Slack notifications from colleagues in different time zones. Edward leaned back, tapped his Mont Blanc pen against the desk, a gift from a deal that had cost three companies their independence, and let out a slow breath. He hated interruptions, especially ones that reminded him of things he'd deliberately forgotten.

His phone buzzed. A WhatsApp message from his sister Hannah: "Freddie says you're being particularly grumpy today. Missing you. xx"

He swiped it away without reading the full message. Family group chats were the digital equivalent of emotional quicksand.

By nine o'clock, the office was empty but for the two of them. The cleaning crew had been and gone. Sloane had switched to a cheaper company that came earlier, cutting corners wherever possible. Edward stood, shrugged on his coat (Burberry, because even misers had standards), and closed his laptop with the satisfaction of a day's profits secured.

"Leave the report on my desk by morning," he said, knowing full well it meant Ben would be there another two hours at least, sustained by energy drinks from the vending machine and the faint hope of a Christmas bonus that would never come.

He descended to the underground car park, the echo of his Italian leather shoes sharp in the cavernous space. His Jaguar F-Type purred awake with the touch of a button, the engine's roar echoing off concrete walls like a mechanical growl. As he drove through the city, Christmas lights blurred past the windscreen like streaks of colour he refused to acknowledge. The radio played carols interrupted by advertisements for cryptocurrency and fast fashion. Carols leaked from pubs where office workers celebrated with drinks they couldn't afford, clusters of young people spilled onto pavements in paper hats, their breath visible in the cold air as they livestreamed their festivities. The air was full of laughter that Edward's sealed windows couldn't quite block out.

His apartment sat high above the river in a converted Victorian warehouse that had been gutted and rebuilt into luxury flats, all glass and chrome, coldly immaculate. Smart home technology responded to his presence, lights dimming to his preferred level, heating adjusting, his Spotify account automatically playing a playlist of minimalist classical music designed to aid concentration. He poured a whisky (Macallan 25, because if you were going to drink alone, you might as well drink well), checked his emails on an iPad propped against the kitchen island, and glanced at the financial news crawling across the bottom of his wall-mounted television screen. Bitcoin was up. Tesla was down. The world kept turning, and Edward Sloane kept profiting.

Everything in its place, everything under control.

And then he froze.

Reflected in the darkened glass of the balcony doors was not his own lean figure but another man's face, pale, hollow-eyed disturbingly familiar. For one dizzying moment, Edward thought he had conjured him out of guilt and memory, but the image did not vanish when he blinked. Jonathan Marks. His old partner. Dead seven years, three months, and sixteen days. Not that Edward was counting.

The whisky trembled in his hand like a leaf in a digital wind. He turned sharply, but the room was empty save for the hum of expensive appliances and the distant sound of traffic. When he looked back at the glass, the face was gone, leaving only his own reflection staring back, older, harder, more alone than he cared to admit.

Edward set down the glass carefully, as if sudden movement might invite something worse. He told himself it was the alcohol, or fatigue, or some trick of the LED lighting. Stress manifested in strange ways. He'd read about it in the Harvard Business Review. But even as he climbed into his king-size bed (Egyptian cotton sheets, changed twice weekly by a cleaning service), the memory of those eyes burned behind his own.

The last thing he saw before sleep took him was his phone screen: 47 unread emails, 12 missed calls, and a notification from his meditation app that he'd ignored for 127 consecutive days.

*

He woke with a start that sent his Apple Watch into cardiac alert mode. The apartment was silent but for the hum of the American-style fridge and the distant whoosh of the building's ventilation system. The whisky glass still stood untouched on the coffee table, amber liquid catching the light from the street. For a moment he thought the vision had been a dream, stress-induced, explicable, nothing that couldn't be solved with a good therapist and better sleep hygiene.

Then came the sound.

Chains, dragging against the imported hardwood floors. Slow, deliberate, each scrape setting his teeth on edge, like fingernails on a smartphone screen. Edward's heart hammered hard enough to trigger another health notification. Nobody could have broken in; the building had keycard access, facial recognition, and security cameras that fed directly to a monitoring company in Milton Keynes. Yet the noise grew louder, closer, rattling like steel against stone, punctuated by a sound that made his blood freeze: the electronic beeping of card machines, the chime of banking apps, the digital symphony of modern commerce.

"Who's there?" he demanded, his voice higher than he intended, echoing off the minimalist walls.

A figure emerged from the shadows of the hallway. At first it seemed like a glitch in his vision, the edges trembling like a corrupted video file, but then it solidified into a man in a tailored suit that had once cost more than most people's cars. His skin was ashen, his eyes hollow but unblinking, and around his body trailed thick chains of a decidedly modern variety: credit cards fused together in endless loops, smartphones with cracked screens, tablets displaying endless spreadsheets, broken Bitcoin mining rigs, contactless payment devices that beeped incessantly. Tangled among them were printed emails, shredded contracts, and what looked like the remains of a Tesla Model S key fob.

Edward stumbled back, clutching his Egyptian cotton duvet. "Marks?"

The ghost inclined his head, lips twisting into something between a LinkedIn profile smile and a grimace of eternal regret.

"You're dead," Edward whispered.

"I am," Jonathan Marks replied. His voice was low, echoing as though carried through an empty trading floor after hours, with the digital distortion of a bad Zoom call. "Dead, and worse than dead. Do you know what it means, Edward, to be bound for eternity by the weight of your own algorithms? Every trade, every optimisation, every human cost deemed 'acceptable loss' forged link by link, app by app, notification by notification." He raised his arms, and the chains rattled with a sound that was part metal, part electronic interference. "I carry the weight of every life I commodified, every worker

I replaced with automation, every small business I helped destroy with market manipulation."

Edward forced a scoff, though it wavered like a bad internet connection. "Hallucination. Stress. That's all this is. Too much whisky. Too many blue screens. I've been spending too much time staring at monitors. Digital eye strain that's what this is."

Marks leaned closer. His breath was cold as server room air conditioning, carrying the metallic tang of copper and thermal paste. "Still clinging to your rational explanations. I was the same in life. Data was my god, growth my salvation, disruption my communion wine. And look at me now. Condemned to carry every byte of human misery I helped create."

The chains around him flickered, and Edward glimpsed images in their surfaces: families evicted by algorithmic rent calculations, gig workers living in cars, teenagers driven to despair by social media metrics they'd helped weaponise.

"I come to warn you, Edward. There is still a chance for you to escape this fate."

"Chance?" Edward sneered, though sweat dampened his temples despite the climate control. "I built this life through data-driven decisions, machine learning optimisation, and strategic automation. Not through ghost stories and Victorian superstition."

"Automation?" The ghost's voice rose, chains clattering violently, the electronic devices sparking and fizzing. "You automated away human dignity. You optimised out compassion. You A/B tested empathy until it failed to show statistical significance. I tell you, Edward, those algorithms will strangle you just as they strangle me."

Edward pressed his palms to his ears, but the voice thundered through the room regardless, seeming to come from every smart device simultaneously.

"I was your partner. We built this empire together, remember? The late nights, the energy drinks, the promise that we'd change the world. You knew me when I still believed we were making things better. Trust me in death: there is no return once the final algorithm executes. Your moral balance sheet bleeds red, and there will be no bailout, no government intervention, no too-big-to-fail salvation."

The words struck harder than any negative review, any market crash. Edward looked at the ghost, at the once-sharp Tom Ford suit now fraying at the digital seams, the glowing chains dragging across the polished concrete floor, the despair in eyes that should no longer exist but somehow held more humanity than they had in life, and something in him faltered.

"Why me?" he whispered. "Why warn me? We weren't even speaking when you... when the heart attack..."

"Because there is still a spark in you," Marks said, and for a moment his voice softened, the digital distortion clearing. "A bit of code that hasn't been corrupted. A chance to debug your life before the system crashes completely. I was not granted that chance. Take it, Edward.

Take it before your humanity gets deprecated and deleted forever."

The ghost straightened, his outline shimmering like a hologram losing signal, beginning to dissolve into pixels.

"Remember what I have said. Expect the first spirit when the clock strikes one. And Edward?"

"What?"

"Delete your meditation app. You're going to need real peace, not the digital kind."

"Don't leave me…" Edward began, but his words were lost in a crash of chains and electronic feedback. The figure shattered like a corrupted video file until only silence remained and the faint smell of overheated processors.

The smart home's LED strips blinked red in sequence, as if the building itself was rebooting. The air conditioning hummed back to life.

Edward sat frozen, sweat chilling on his back despite the perfect climate control, every nerve alive with terror. He wanted to believe it was a dream, a stress-induced hallucination brought on by too much screen time and processed food. But on the polished concrete floor, lying across the underfloor heating like discarded cable, was a single length of broken chain, made not of iron, but of fused credit cards, their magnetic strips forming links that caught the ambient light from his router.

He didn't touch it. He couldn't. His hands shook as he reached for his phone instead, muscle memory seeking comfort in the familiar weight of connected technology.

Instead, he poured another whisky with trembling fingers, sat in the dark surrounded by the soft glow of standby lights and charging indicators, and waited for the clock to strike one.

His phone displayed the time in crisp, digital certainty: 00:47.

Thirteen minutes until his life changed forever.

CHAPTER TWO:

The Spirit of Christmas Past

The flat was so quiet that even the router's
LED pulse seemed like a heartbeat, the
only sound in a world holding its breath.
Edward sat on the edge of his bed, glass
untouched beside him, watching the clock
on his phone tick its way toward digital
destiny. 00:58. 00:59.

He told himself he'd imagined
everything. The face in the glass. The
chains. The cold grip of dread. He
rehearsed plausible explanations like a

start-up pitch: overtiredness, a documentary half-watched on Netflix, the whisky mixing badly with his blood pressure medication. The mind makes deepfakes of memory; he thought. It renders fear in shapes that seem real until you examine the source code.

The digits turned.

01:00.

The sound did not come from his phone or the digital clock on the bedside table or the smart home's speakers. It came from everywhere at once: a single, bell-clear chime that seemed to emanate from time itself, as if someone had struck a tuning fork against the fabric of reality. Light spilled into the room, not the blue glow of screens or the warm yellow of smart bulbs, but something older, analogue, the kind of light that existed before electricity, before pixels, before the world learned to measure everything in megabytes and market shares.

"Edward," said a voice, low and perfectly calm, with the warmth of a human speaking face-to-face rather than through a screen. "It's time to go offline."

A figure stood at the foot of the bed. They were neither young nor old, or rather they were both. Age moving across them like frames in a slideshow. For a heartbeat Edward saw a woman in a 1980s Fair Isle jumper, her hair feathered in a style that predated social media; then a tall youth in a school blazer, hair falling into eyes unmarked by the blue light fatigue that plagued his generation; then a person in a simple white shirt with sleeves rolled to the elbow, the fabric glowing softly as if lit from within, untouched by the planned obsolescence that governed everything else.

The face was kind and grave and not to be argued with, the face of someone who had never needed to curate their image for public consumption.

"You are the first," Edward said, surprised by how steady he sounded. "Christmas Past."

"I am," the spirit replied. Their breath misted, though the room's climate control maintained a constant 21 degrees Celsius. "Walk with me. Leave your devices behind."

"I'm not dressed," he muttered, looking down at his old university T-shirt and the joggers he'd ordered online without trying on. "And I need my phone. What if there's an emergency? What if the markets…"

"You are dressed enough for memory," the spirit said, and reached out. Their hand was not a hand at all but a seam of light, warm as a candle held near the skin, analogue in a digital world. When it touched his shoulder, the apartment folded with the soft hiss of paper being turned, the glass and chrome thinning like a webpage being closed, the smart home's hum fading, the bed sliding away beneath him like a deleted file.

Edward did not fall. He stood. Air bit his cheeks, real air, not filtered and purified, and the smell of wet wool and floor polish and oranges pressed itself into his lungs. Sound blossomed: high laughter, the squeal of trainers on varnished wood, the thin clang of a radiator that never quite worked and couldn't be controlled by an app.

The world focused, rendering like an old photograph developing in a darkroom

The primary school playground of his childhood appeared, perfect as a photograph but more real than any Instagram filter had ever made the present seem.

And the spirit led him into his past.

Edward stood stiffly, hands curled into fists that had never learned to swipe or tap, the cold biting his skin with the honesty of weather that couldn't be adjusted by algorithm. He wanted to believe this was still some elaborate VR simulation, a hallucination brought on by too much screen time and too little human contact. Yet the warmth of the spirit's touch lingered, and the schoolyard stretched before him with merciless clarity.

The playground was just as he remembered, but somehow more vivid than memory usually allowed: red-brick walls stained with decades of rain, iron railings painted in chipping green that had been applied by human hands rather than automated spray systems, puddles frozen into slick mirrors that reflected a sky unmarked by drone traffic. Children in thick coats ran and shrieked, their breath steaming in air that had never been filtered through HEPA systems. They played games with rules passed down through generations of playground democracy, no apps required.

The smell of wet wool and floor polish struck him like a blow from a simpler time. It was the last day of term before Christmas, 1983, and every child ran to waiting parents armed with film cameras rather than smartphones.

Except one.

The boy stood alone, parka zipped up to his chin, one glove a different colour to the other, hand-me-downs, clearly, from a time when everything wasn't disposable. His shoes were scuffed Clarks, the kind you could get resoled rather than replaced. His hair was too long, as though no one had bothered to book him an appointment for months, and there was something in his posture that spoke of resilience learned too young. He looked left, then right, hope flickering in his eyes with every passing Ford Escort and

Austin Metro, cars built to last rather than to require constant upgrades.

Edward knew exactly how long that hope lasted. He had lived it.

"My father was late," he said aloud. His voice cracked in the cold, sounding younger than it had in decades. "He wasn't coming."

The spirit gave no reply, only watched with eyes that had seen this scene play out countless times across countless lives.

The boy waited until the playground emptied, until even the teachers had gone home to their own families and their own celebrations. Then, with the sag of someone older than his seven years, he ducked through the gap in the fence and trudged home along the icy path, his breath visible in the air like small ghosts of disappointed hope.

Edward followed, though part of him wanted to run in the opposite direction. The memory moved with dreamlike precision through streets that hadn't yet been surveilled by CCTV, past shops with hand-painted signs rather than LED displays: the corner newsagent with its bell that rang when you opened the door, the chippy that still wrapped food in yesterday's newspaper, the post office that knew everyone's name.

They reached the terraced house where Edward had grown up, smaller than he remembered, shabbier, but somehow more real than his current glass tower. The front door stuck because the wood had swollen with damp, not because it needed a security update. The kitchen was too quiet, filled with the analogue silence of a house where no devices hummed or beeped or demanded attention.

On the Formica counter, a note written in biro on the back of an envelope:

Working late. Sausage and chips in oven. Be good, E. Dad

No mobile phones to send a quick text. No GPS to track delays. Just the brutal honesty of absence.

The boy, himself all those years ago, ate one cold sausage standing up, put the rest back, and wandered the house in silence. With no tablets to distract him, no streaming services to numb the loneliness. In his bedroom, he stood in front of the mirror and whispered the line he would have spoken at the school concert: "Good evening, ladies and gentlemen..." He bowed to no one, then crawled into bed i his jumper, because the heating was on a timer and the blanket was thin, and the house was never warm enough.

Edward reached for the bed, his hand passing through the faded Superman duvet cover. His throat tightened with emotions he'd spent decades learning to suppress. "I had forgotten this," he said.

"No," the spirit replied softly. "You archived it. Compressed it. Tried to delet it. But the file was never truly gone."

The room pixelated and reformed, the plain bedroom walls dissolving into a school gym lit with paper chains rather than programmable LEDs. Folding chair squeaked under the weight of parents armed with Kodak cameras, their flashes popping like tiny supernovae. At the back, a girl stood on tiptoes, straining to see over the crowd.

"Hannah," Edward breathed. His younger sister, plaits bouncing, cheeks pink with excitement and cold air. She darted through the crowd to him, schoolbag thumping her side. From it she produced a cheese sandwich wrapped in cling film, still warm from being carried close to her body.

"Dad's not coming," she said with a shrug that tried to be casual but couldn't quite hide the hurt. "So what? We'll clap loud enough for three people. And I saved you half my lunch."

She pressed the sandwich into his hands with the fierce love of an eight-year-old who understood injustice but refused to let it win.

Edward made a sound that was neither laugh nor sob, recognising in his sister's gesture the template for every act of kindness he'd since learned to dismiss as inefficient. The spirit's hand hovered at his shoulder but did not touch.

"Come," it said. "There is more data to recover."

*

The scene shifted like a webpage loading, the school gym dissolving into the fogged windows of a student pub circa 1998. Edward found himself watching a younger version of himself laugh beside a girl with a scarf dotted like stars and eyes that sparkled with more life than any display screen. Bella James.

She was everything his algorithmic world would later reject as unpredictable: bright, impulsive, endlessly curious about things that couldn't be monetised. They shared chips stolen from each other's plates, browsed second-hand bookshops for hours without buying anything, sang along to the radio in voices that were beautifully, humanly imperfect. They had almost nothing, student loans, overdrafts, a shared mobile phone that could barely send text messages, and they were richer than Edward would ever be again.

"Look at yourself," the spirit said gently. "Before you learned to optimise happiness out of existence."

Edward felt the old warmth flood back, so strong it hurt worse than any market crash. The young man in the pub was laughing at something Bella had said, not checking his phone, not calculating ROI on the evening, just present in a way that seemed impossible now.

"Stop here," he begged the spirit. "Let me stay in this moment. Before I…"

But the spirit would not stop. Time accelerated, frames skipping like a corrupted video file.

The lights changed. Bella stood beneath fairy lights in the same pub three years later, two takeaway coffee cups in her hands. Edward was there too, older now, his first proper suit pinching his shoulders, a BlackBerry glowing on the table between them like a digital chaperone.

"I want what's best for us," he said. His tone was clipped, rehearsed, like every presentation he'd perfected since joining the graduate trainee program.

"You want what's safest for your career trajectory," Bella replied, not angry, just tired in a way that seemed to age her before his eyes. "Which, as it happens, is the same as what will make you loneliest."

She set down the coffees and walked away, her star-patterned scarf trailing behind her like a discarded constellation. The young Edward watched her go, then immediately picked up his BlackBerry to check emails, using work as a digital anaesthetic for the pain he couldn't quite process.

Edward closed his eyes, but the memory continued behind his eyelids with high-definition cruelty. He remembered every pixel of that moment.

*

The scene unravelled like deleted browser history. Offices sprouted in its place: glass doors, strip lighting that hummed with electronic efficiency, his name etched on frosted panels in fonts chosen by brand consultants. Deals struck via video call. Emails sent at midnight from hotel rooms in cities that all looked the same. Hannah's calls were answered with increasing brevity, then declined, then blocked when she persisted in trying to maintain what he'd learned to see as an inefficient emotional overhead.

Christmases reduced to same-day delivery gift cards purchased via app. Phone calls trimmed to quarterly check-ins, then annual, then archived as "legacy contacts." Ambition grew fat on productivity apps while relationships starved on digital neglect.

Edward tried to speak, but the words were compressed, unplayable.

The spirit raised a hand. A new scene buffered into existence: a front garden with fairy lights that blinked in patterns no algorithm had optimised, hedges trimmed by human hands. Inside, through windows uncovered by smart blinds, Hannah laughed with her son while they decorated gingerbread men with wonky icing smiles. Warmth spilled through the glass like an analogue stream of contentment.

Edward stepped toward the warmth, reaching for the door, but his hand passed through like light through a hologram. He was an observer, forever locked out of the human network he'd spent years learning to see as inefficient.

He turned to the spirit. "Have I seen enough? Can we close this session?"

"No." Its voice was steady, neither cruel nor kind, like a system administrator delivering facts. "You must see the final output of your optimisation choices."

The light folded again, compressed and re-compressed until they stood in the Carter flat. Edward recognised it from the background of Ben's Zoom calls, small but warm, filled with the beautiful chaos of human life unmanaged by productivity apps. Mismatched plates set for Christmas dinner, children darting about like packets of unstructured data, their mother bustling to keep them fed without the aid of smart home automation.

At the centre sat Toby, paper crown askew, smile so wide it looked like defiance against a world that would soon teach him to commodify joy. His laugh was pure warmth, unfiltered and unprocessed.

Edward leaned forward, aching to hug the boy, to say something kind, anything that might serve as antivirus software for the loneliness he saw approaching. But the spirit's eyes, grave and knowing, held him back.

"Why show me this?" Edward demanded, his voice glitching with emotion. "This is the present, not the past. This data doesn't belong in this dataset."

"Every present," said the spirit, downloading wisdom in packets Edward's heart could barely process, "is a past in the making. Every moment you choose efficiency over humanity becomes tomorrow's regret.exe."

Toby coughed then. Just a cough, but it lingered one beat too long, like a system error that suggested deeper corruption. Edward felt the sound echo inside his chest like feedback through badly configured speakers.

"Enough," he whispered. "Please. End the session."

The spirit inclined its head. The flat dissolved into shadows, folding back into

Edward's apartment like a browser window being closed. The router blinked, the digital clock glowed, the smart home hummed back to electronic life. The spirit stood at the foot of his bed once more, already beginning to fade like a video call losing connection.

"You have seen what you were, and what you lost," it said. "Remember: some files, once deleted, cannot be recovered."

The surrounding light dimmed, leaving only cold air and the gentle buzz of standby mode.

Edward looked at the clock. 01:59.

His heart rate spiked as the Apple Watch registered his stress. Another hour was loading, and he was afraid the next spirit would show him data he wasn't ready to process.

CHAPTER THREE:

The Spirit of Christmas Present

Edward's sleep was fragmented, interrupted by notification alerts that seemed to come from inside his dreams. He woke with a jolt as his fitness tracker registered REM cycle completion, heart thudding against ribs that felt too thin, too fragile. He had no memory of falling back asleep, yet the night had advanced without him, time passing like data through fibre optic cables, invisible, instantaneous, irreversible.

The apartment glowed strangely, not with the blue wash of LED strips or the targeted illumination of smart bulbs responding to presence sensors, but with something warmer, richer, more alive. It was the kind of light that existed before energy efficiency ratings, before circadian rhythm optimisation, before anyone thought to patent the spectrum of human comfort.

From the kitchen came laughter. Not the curated laughter of social media videos or the processed chuckles of streaming comedy, but deep and round and real, the kind that filled a room like steam from a kettle, like sound waves uncompressed by digital algorithms.

Edward pulled himself from the bed, feet hitting the polished concrete floor that his smart home's sensors immediately registered, adjusting ambient temperature and lighting in response. But the automatic systems seemed somehow subdued, as if even his technology recognised the presence of something more powerful.

He followed the sound, padding barefoot past walls of glass and chrome that had cost more per square meter than most people earned in a year.

The sight that met him rewrote his understanding of his own space.

His sleek, sterile kitchen had been transformed into something from a different era, a different algorithm entirely. The minimalist surfaces had vanished beneath evergreen boughs strung with ribbons that looked hand-tied rather than mass-produced. Fairy lights twinkled, not programmable LEDs responding to voice commands, but simple incandescent bulbs that cast warm shadows and consumed electricity with joyful inefficiency.

Platters of food covered the granite counters: roasted meats that smelled of real ovens rather than smart appliances, steaming puddings that had never seen a recipe app, oranges studded with cloves in patterns that followed tradition rather than trending hashtags. Bottles of wine gleamed, not expensive vintages chosen by algorithm but honest bottles that promised conversation rather than status. The air smelled of spice and heat and comfort, of time taken rather than time saved.

In the centre stood a giant of a figure, draped in a green robe trimmed with fur that had never been processed through sustainable supply chain optimisation. Their beard was thick and real, untrimmed by precision grooming apps, their eyes merry with the kind of happiness that couldn't be measured in engagement metrics. Upon their brow sat a wreath of holly, its berries red as notification badges but infinitely more alive.

Around them, abundance spilled like data from a generously configured server, not the curated abundance of Edward's portfolio, but the messy, joyful overflow of human generosity.

Edward swallowed. "You must be the second spirit."

"I am the Spirit of Christmas Present!" the figure boomed, voice rolling like surround sound through the transformed space. "Come closer, man. See the world as it uploads in real time, unfiltered and uncompressed."

The spirit clapped Edward on the back so hard he nearly staggered, the impact more real than any haptic feedback he'd ever experienced. Then, with a sweep of its hand that scattered light like pixels reassembling, the room dissolved into pure connection.

*

The City in Celebration

They stood on the streets of London, but not the London Edward knew from his tinted car windows and climate-controlled offices. Snowflakes swirled in the air, each one unique as a hand-coded solution, the pavements busy with families carrying bags of food they'd chosen themselves rather than ordered through delivery apps. Market stalls bustled with last-minute shoppers who touched and smelled and tasted, engaging their senses in ways that no e-commerce interface could replicate.

Children pulled sledges that had been handed down through generations rather than ordered from Amazon. Their laughter echoed off buildings that predated social media, their joy unmonetised and untracked.

From every pub and café, music and chatter spilled into the streets, not curated playlists or algorithmic recommendations, but the random, beautiful chaos of human voices mixing like open-source code written by a thousand different programmers.

Edward had walked these streets countless times, but always inside vehicles or lost in phone screens, never seeing them like this. People smiled at strangers without checking their follower counts. Doors stood open with wreaths hanging bright, welcoming everyone rather than just verified users. Even those who had little seemed to share it freely, their generosity unconditioned by reward schemes or loyalty programs.

"See them," the spirit said, its voice carrying the warmth of a server room before the fans kicked in. "Everywhere, joy. Not because their bank statements are optimised, but because they choose to run a different program today. Can you not feel the network effect?"

Edward felt it, though he hated to admit it. The warmth pressed against his chest like data trying to install itself, but so too did a sharp pang of envy, the recognition that he'd spent years building walls against this very connection.

A group of teenagers walked past, phones tucked away, singing carols with voices that cracked and soared without auto-tune. An elderly man fed pigeons from a paper bag, talking to them like old friends. A mother pushed a buggy while her toddler pointed at lights with a wonder that no app could simulate.

"This is inefficient," Edward muttered, but his voice lacked conviction. "They're wasting time, energy. No productivity metrics, no ROI measurement."

The spirit's laugh rumbled like a server booting up. "And yet their happiness metrics are off the charts. Curious, isn't it?"

*

The Hospital

The scene shifted with the smooth transition of a well-coded interface. Now Edward stood in a hospital children's ward, where technology served humanity rather than replacing it. Monitors beeped with the rhythm of small hearts, but they were background music to something more important.

Tinsel looped along the walls, hand-cut paper snowflakes dangled from strings held by Blu-Tac rather than smart adhesives. Nurses wore Santa hats over their scrubs, moving quickly but gently, carrying trays of hot drinks that steamed with human warmth. The Wi-Fi here was reliable but rarely used; children preferred analogue play.

Children in pyjamas that had been washed a hundred times unwrapped donated gifts, their eyes wide with delight that no algorithm could predict or replicate. These weren't targeted recommendations based on browsing history, but surprises chosen by human hearts.

One little girl hugged a doll as if it were the greatest treasure in the world, her embrace worth more than any in-app purchase. Another boy laughed as a nurse pushed him in a wheelchair decorated with fairy lights powered by battery packs rather than smart home systems. Parents sat close to their children, holding their hands as if nothing else mattered, no phones visible, no status updates shared.

Edward looked around at the weary bu glowing faces and felt something crack in his chest. "I've donated to hospitals," he said, as if reading from his tax return. "M name's on plaques. The Edward Sloane Foundation for Paediatric Technology."

The spirit bent low, its eyes fierce despite the smile. "Data without presence is only half a transaction. Money without touch is cryptocurrency, valuable on paper, worthless for warmth. These families upload something that can't be quantified. They give their authenticated selves."

A young father sat beside a tiny bed, reading "The Gruffalo" in a voice hoarse from hours of storytelling. His daughter's

eyes never left his face, downloading love
in real time through fibre optic
connections older than the internet.

Edward said nothing. His throat felt
compressed.

*

The Carters' Christmas

The warmth of the ward folded away
into the modest Carter flat, data packets
reassembling into Edward's most familiar
anxiety. He recognised the space instantly
from Zoom backgrounds and the
occasional glimpse through Ben's
exhausted updates. It was cramped, the
wallpaper tired, the furniture assembled
from flat-pack instructions. But the
atmosphere glowed with a life that no
smart home system could generate.

On the dining table sat a bird that was trying its best to be turkey, potatoes crisped in an oven that predated smart appliances, crackers ready to pull, the kind that came with plastic toys and terrible jokes, unoptimised for anything except joy. Children darted about in paper hats that had cost pence but delivered more satisfaction than any premium subscription.

Ben's wife orchestrated it all with weary cheer, smiling despite the strain that showed in the dark circles under her eyes, the tremor in her hands as she carried dishes that were mismatched but full of love. She moved like a systems administrator keeping a failing server running through sheer determination.

At the centre of it all sat Toby, his paper crown sliding over his brow like a user interface element refusing to stay positioned. His cheeks were pale, his frame too thin, yet his grin was wide enough to light the room better than any LED array. He clutched a small tablet that was several generations old, but he wasn't staring at the screen; he was watching his family, downloading their happiness through biological bandwidth.

Edward stared at him, throat tight with uncompressed emotion.

"Remarkable, isn't it?" the spirit said gently. "A child running on limited processing power, and yet he makes the entire system brighter."

"He looks..." Edward's voice caught like a program hitting an exception. "The cough. He's still coughing."

The spirit's face grew grave, its jolly expression buffering into something sadder. "If the current parameters remain unchanged, the boy will encounter a fatal error. His system won't see another Christmas."

Edward spun, desperate. "No. That can't be the output. He's just a child. Can't you patch it? Fix the bug?"

The spirit shook its head with the slow inevitability of a security update that couldn't be postponed. "Your world measures value in quarterly reports. But his value, his laughter, his love, his wonder, exists in formats your balance sheets can't read. Still, unless someone updates the code, inputs new variables, he will be lost."

Edward's eyes stung with the salt of emotions he hadn't processed in years. He reached toward Toby, wanting to touch him, to transfer something, hope, health, happiness, but his hand passed through like light through fibre-optic cable, carrying information but unable to make physical contact.

Ben Carter raised his glass of supermarket prosecco. "To family," he said. His voice cracked like an overloaded audio codec, but he smiled anyway, love overriding the system errors. The children cheered, plastic cups of juice clinking together in analogue harmony.

Edward turned away, unable to watch this beautiful inefficiency, this glorious waste of resources that somehow generated more value than all his optimised algorithms.

*

Freddie's Party

The scene blurred like a transition effect, reassembling into Freddie's flat in Camden. The place was crowded with twenty-somethings who still believed in making the world better rather than just more profitable. Fairy lights were strung haphazardly, not part of any smart lighting scheme, but wound around banisters and doorframes with the chaotic creativity of analogue minds.

Music pulsed from speakers that were decent but not audiophile grade, carrying songs that prioritised feeling over perfect sound reproduction. Friends in paper hats lounged on battered sofas held together by hope and gaffer tape, balancing plates of roast potatoes that had been cooked b trial and error rather than precise temperature control, wine glasses filled from bottles chosen for fun labels rather than investment potential.

Freddie himself, in a Santa hat that had seen better decades, darted about like a friendly virus spreading joy through the network. He topped up drinks, hugged people with the abandon of someone who'd never learned to quantify social energy, laughed so hard tears streamed down his face in displays of emotion that would never trend on TikTok but were infinitely more valuable.

Edward stood at the doorway, invisible but aching like a phantom limb syndrome of the heart. He had been invited to this party every year through carefully crafted text messages and voicemails left with genuine hope, and every year he had declined with automated responses about prior commitments. Now he saw the empty chair kept by the window, positioned to catch both light and conversation. A plate waited with crackers and paper crowns, a place setting for an uncle who existed in theory but never in practice.

"He left space in the RAM," the spirit said softly. "Allocated memory for you, kept the connection open even when you kept refusing to handshake."

Edward pressed his hand to the frame of the doorway, feeling the wood grain under his fingertips, a real texture that no haptic feedback could replicate. For the first time in years, he longed to step inside, to sit at that table, to authenticate himself as part of this human network. To belong to something more valuable than a portfolio.

But the scene spun away before he could initiate contact, leaving him with the error message of regret.

*

The Spirit's Warning

They were back in the street, but the atmosphere had changed like weather data updating in real time. Snow fell heavier now, muffling the city's hum with the silence that came before digital noise. The spirit towered above Edward, its face still merry, but shadows clung to its robe like corrupted data files.

"Are spirits' lives so short?" Edward asked suddenly, noticing how the figure seemed already older, its features dimming like a screen losing brightness. "Do you run on limited battery?"

"My runtime is brief," the spirit said, voice beginning to distort like a connection failing. "My process terminates at midnight. But before I power down, you must see this final output."

From the folds of its robe emerged two figures, small and twisted, crouching like malware hiding in system files. They moved with a jerky, unnatural motion of artificial intelligence trying to mimic human behaviour but failing to capture the essence.

One was gaunt, eyes hollow, gnawing on invisible data scraps like a program forever searching for resources. The other was sharp-boned, snarling, clutching tight to what little it had like a user hoarding storage space on a failing hard drive.

Edward recoiled, recognising something familiar in their digital desperation. "What are they? Some kind of virus?"

"This boy is Ignorance. This girl is Want," the spirit said gravely, its voice now carrying the static of a poor connection. "They are the offspring of your world's favourite algorithm, the one that optimises for profit over people, efficiency over empathy. They cling to mankind like spyware, growing stronger with every human connection severed, every community disbanded for better margins."

The two figures hissed at Edward, their eyes reflecting the cold light of screens rather than the warmth of human souls.

"Beware them both," the spirit continued, its image beginning to pixelate, "but most of all beware Ignorance, for on his brow I see doom written in code that cannot be debugged."

Edward shook his head, hands making the gesture of dismissing a pop-up window. "Can nothing be done? No patch, no update?"

"Can anything be done when the primary users of your platform choose to look away?" the spirit asked, its voice now distant like a call from a satellite with a failing orbit. "When the administrators prioritise engagement metrics over human welfare?"

Before Edward could reply, the clock struck again, not the gentle chime of his phone, but the deep, resonant tone of time itself marking another hour passed. The spirit's laugh, once joyous, now sounded like audio compression artefacts, hollow and distorted. Its form flickered like a video stream buffering over a slow connection, then dissolved into static, leaving only the ghost of its presence in the air.

Edward was alone once more, his apartment cold and silent except for the hum of electronic devices in standby mode, the gentle ping of notifications from a world that never slept, never stopped demanding his attention.

The clock read 02:59.

Another process was about to launch. And Edward was afraid this next application would show him outputs that would crash his system entirely.

CHAPTER FOUR:

The Spirit of Christmas Yet to Come

Edward lay frozen in bed, though the smart home's climate control maintained optimal sleeping temperature. His Apple Watch recorded an elevated heart rate, interrupted sleep patterns, stress indicators off the charts, data points that would normally trigger a consultation reminder from his health app. But tonight, the notifications seemed trivial compared to the weight of dread that pressed against his chest like a failing server about to crash.

———— ✳ ————

The air felt different, heavier, denser, as if the very atmosphere had been compressed into a smaller file size. The usual electronic hum of his life, the Wi-Fi router, the smart fridge, the charging stations, all seemed muted, running in background mode.

And then it came.

The shadow rose at the foot of his bed, taller than the ceiling, darker than any display when the power failed. It was less a presence than an absence, a void in the shape of something that had once been human but had been stripped of every inefficient component, every unnecessary subroutine of mercy or hope.

It said nothing. No voice synthesis, no audio output. It lifted only one pale hand, the finger pointing forward with the inexorable command of a system administrator directing a user to face their final account audit.

Edward swung his legs from the bed, feet hitting the cold floor that immediately registered his presence and adjusted the lighting accordingly, but the automated responses seemed weak, overwhelmed by something that operated on older, more fundamental protocols.

His voice cracked like a corrupted audio file. "Spirit, I fear you more than the others, but I will go. If there's any hope left for me, any possibility of system recovery, I must know."

The ghost did not move, but the walls of the bedroom peeled back like layers of an onion being stripped away, or files being deleted from a drive. Edward stumbled forward into the world, feeling like a user being transferred from a familiar interface into something alien and unforgiving.

*

The City Without Him

They stood in the financial district, but it looked different now, sharper, colder, more automated. The buildings rose like server towers, their windows glowing with the blue light of screens rather than the warm yellow of human habitation. Digital billboards flashed with stock prices and cryptocurrency values, but no advertisements for things people needed.

A group of brokers huddled outside a coffee kiosk, their conversation carrying on the cold air like data packets over a network.

"Did you hear about Sloane?" one said, scrolling through his phone rather than making eye contact.

The others looked up from their devices with the mild interest of users consuming disposable content.

"Dead last week. Heart attack, apparently. Guess all those energy drinks and eighteen-hour days finally caught up with him."

"Good riddance," another said, already losing interest, thumb moving to refresh his feed. "Man was a nightmare to work for. Only cared about numbers. Treated humans like deprecated hardware."

A third shrugged, typing while talking. "He had money, though. Bet he left a fortune. Wonder who inherits the algorithms?"

"Fortune's only worth something if there's someone left who gives a shit you're gone," the first replied, already walking away, attention captured by a notification. "Anyway, did you see the crypto crash this morning? There's real money to be made in the dip."

They dispersed like a disbanded chat room, each absorbed in their individual screens, already forgetting him.

Edward's throat closed like a program terminating unexpectedly. "Spirit... is this me? Are they talking about me?"

The ghost only raised its hand, pointing on with the relentless logic of code executing its instructions.

*

The Abandoned Office

Edward found himself outside the glass tower of Sloane & Marks LLP, but the building looked different now, abandoned, like a website that had been taken offline. The LED sign was dark, with some letters missing, giving it the appearance of corrupted text. Windows that had once blazed with the activity of human ambition now stared blank and dark.

Inside, the desks stood empty like decommissioned workstations. Dust filmed the screens of computers that would never boot again. Plants withered in the corners; their smart watering systems having failed when the maintenance contracts expired. The open-plan office looked like a data centre after a complete system failure.

He walked into the boardroom, where he had made his most ruthless decisions. The oak table was scratched, chairs overturned, whiteboards still showing the ghost of presentations about optimisation and efficiency. Papers lay scattered on the floor like printouts from a crashed printer.

A cleaner moved through the space with the methodical efficiency of an automated system, gathering discarded electronics. She opened a drawer and pulled out a watch, his watch, the expensive one he swapped for his Apple Watch to signal success to the few he wished to impress.

"Nice bit of tech," she muttered, slipping it into her pocket like salvaging components from a broken device.

Edward spun to the spirit. "They're stealing! This is my data, my assets!"

The figure did not answer, its silence as final as a computer that refuses to respond to user input.

"This can't be my legacy. Not like this."

The ghost pointed toward the window. Outside, the skyline of London glowed coldly, its lights following algorithmic patterns that cared nothing for the humans who had once given them meaning.

*

The Carters' Home

The scene shifted abruptly, reality reformatting like a hard drive being wiped and reloaded. Edward staggered as the world reassembled into the Carter flat.

But it was different. The space felt deflated, like a balloon losing air, or a system running in safe mode with all non essential processes disabled. The family photos were turned face down. The television showed only static. The Christmas decorations had been packed away, leaving pale rectangles on the walls where they had hung.

The table was bare. No crackers, no laughter, no sound of children playing games that required nothing more than imagination. The silence was digital in its completeness, not the natural quiet of rest, but the absence of all that made the space alive.

Ben sat hunched in a chair that had seen better years, face pale as a monitor displaying only white, hands clasped as if trying to hold on to something that kept slipping away. His wife moved quietly in the kitchen, red-eyed from crying, going through motions that had lost their meaning. The other children played half-heartedly with toys that seemed to have lost their capacity for joy.

And then Edward saw it.

In the corner leaned a crutch, small, unused, abandoned like hardware for a user who had logged off permanently.

"No," Edward whispered, his voice barely above the level of a failing speaker. "Tell me it's not true. Tell me the boy still runs. Tell me his process hasn't terminated."

The figure did not move, its silence carrying the weight of a system error that could not be resolved.

Edward dropped to his knees on the cheap carpet, feeling the static electricity of synthetic fibres. "Please. I'll change the algorithm. I'll rewrite the code. I'll do anything. Just restore from backup."

Still, the figure was silent, like a help desk that had been permanently closed.

The Funeral

The flat dissolved, leaving only cold earth beneath Edward's knees like a computer crashing and dumping him to a command line interface. He was in a graveyard, frost whitening the grass like pixels on a corrupted screen. A small knot of mourners stood around an open grave, most of them checking their phones rather than paying attention to the service.

A vicar muttered words from a tablet, bored, glancing at his smartwatch as if calculating the minimum time required for this particular subroutine. His delivery was robotic, processed through years of similar functions until humanity had been compressed out of it entirely.

Edward forced his way forward, though he knew they could not see him, he was a ghost in his own life's final scene. He stared down at the coffin, its surface reflecting the grey sky like a powered-down screen. The brass nameplate read only:

Edward Sloane
1968–2025
Connection Lost

No epitaph. No "beloved" or "missed." No user comments, no five-star ratings, no indication that this life had touched others. Just a name, dates, and the notification that the system had failed to maintain contact.

Edward clutched the edge of the grave, feeling the cold earth crumble under his fingers like a database corruption spreading through a network. "Spirit! This is me. But it must be a warning, not a final error. Tell me there's still hope for system recovery!"

The spirit raised its hand once more, pointing down into the digital void. Darkness swelled, pouring into Edward's chest like malware installing itself in core system files until he could hardly breathe.

"Please!" he cried, his voice echoing like audio feedback in an empty server room. "I don't want this output. I will update the program. I will live differently. Only give me administrative privileges!"

The hand did not move. The earth crumbled beneath him like a failing hard drive. He felt himself falling into the coffin, the lid closing above him like a laptop shutting down for the final time.

And then he screamed, the sound carrying across the graveyard like a dial-up modem trying to connect to a network that no longer existed.

*

Colleagues Divide the Spoils

The scream dissolved into the ambient noise of the city, reformatting into the familiar hum of voices in a corporate environment. Edward blinked, finding himself in a trendy coffee shop near Bank station, the kind with exposed brick walls and baristas who could recite the origin story of every bean.

Three men and a woman in sharp suits sat with laptops open, the screens reflecting their faces in blue light. Their conversation mixed with the sound of espresso machines and the gentle ping of notifications.

"Funny, isn't it?" one said, not looking up from his trading app. "All those years Sloane kept everything locked down. Wouldn't share access credentials with anyone. Digital hoarder. And now? Free-for-all on his assets."

They laughed, the hollow laughter of people who had learned to find humour in other people's tragedies, monetising grief into opportunities.

"The portfolio's already been liquidated," the woman said, scrolling through financial news. "Market absorbed it without a blip. Just another data point in the algorithm."

"Imagine dedicating your entire life to accumulating digital wealth," said the third, pausing his game of mobile solitaire. "And then having it disappear faster than a deleted tweet. No legacy, no lasting impact."

"Not even a decent obituary," added the first. "Just a press release from the company. 'Edward Sloane, CEO, has disconnected from our network. His user account has been deactivated.' That's it."

Edward shouted, "That's not true! I built this company! I changed the industry!" But they could not hear him, he was speaking to a system that had already deleted his user profile.

The spirit pointed toward the door with the inexorable logic of a redirect command.

Freddie's Grief

Now Edward was in Freddie's flat, but the warmth had been drained from it like colour from an old photograph. The fairy lights still hung, but half had burned out and not been replaced. The tree stood bare, its smart lights having lost connection to the home network.

Freddie sat at the table, head in his hands, looking older than his years. His phone lay face down, an unusual sight for someone of his generation. "I tried," he said to his partner, who hovered nearby like tech support trying to console a user whose system had crashed. "Inviting him, keeping the virtual door open. But he never logged in. He never cared about anything that couldn't be monetised."

His partner touched his arm, an analogue gesture of comfort that no app could replicate. "He was who he was. You can't debug someone else's personality."

Freddie looked up, eyes wet with the kind of tears that would never become content for social media. "But he was my uncle. My family. I didn't want him to die alone, disconnected from everything that mattered."

Edward pressed his hand to the window, desperate to break through the barrier between them, to send some signal that he was here, that he understood now. "Freddie, I'm here. I care now. Can you see me? Can you hear my transmission?" But the glass was solid, offering no connection protocol.

The spirit loomed behind him, a presence like a server room moments before the power failed completely.

*

The Lonely Flat

They were back in Edward's own apartment, but it was no longer the pristine smart home he had cultivated. Dust covered every surface like neglected cache files. Newspapers piled by the door, their headlines growing increasingly irrelevant as time passed. The blinds hung askew, their automated systems having failed without maintenance.

The smart home's various sensors blinked red in the darkness, error codes indicating system failures throughout the network. The voice assistant sat silent, its wake word no longer recognised because no one was there to speak it. Plants had died in their self-watering containers; the technology having failed when the subscription service expired.

On the coffee table sat a half-empty bottle of whisky that had gathered dust like an artefact from a lost civilisation. The air smelled stale, like a data centre with failed ventilation.

In the bedroom, the sheets were grey with dust and neglect. The bed hadn't been slept in for years; the smart mattress still tracked sleep patterns for a user who would never return, its data growing increasingly meaningless as time passed.

Edward shuddered, recognising the fate of all systems without maintenance, all networks without human connection.

"This... this is how they'll find me? Alone in a failed smart home?"

Rats scurried across the floor, their claws scratching against surfaces that had once been kept pristine by automated cleaning systems. They had made nests in the expensive electronics, finding warmth in devices that would never boot again.

Edward recoiled. "No. Not like this. Not as a cautionary tale about the dangers of digital isolation."

*

The Final Vision

The graveyard materialised around them once more, but this time, no mourners remained. Just an open, unmarked grave that looked like a hole in the world's database. Rain dripped into the pit, each drop creating tiny craters in the earth like pixels dying on a screen.

The headstone had weathered badly, its text becoming illegible like data corruption spreading through storage media. Soon, even his name would be unreadable.

Edward dropped to his knees, feeling the cold mud soak through his pyjamas. "Spirit, I understand now. This is the output if I continue running the same algorithm. But I am not a deprecated system. Please, give me a chance to rewrite the code."

The figure loomed above, silent as a crashed computer, its hand pointing once more at the grave with the relentless logic of a program executing its final instruction.

Edward clutched at the shadow, his hands passing through like trying to grasp data made manifest. "I will change! I will live differently! I'll prioritise human connections over digital metrics! Only tell me these visions are warnings, not inevitable outcomes!"

The hand trembled, or did it? Perhaps it was just visual artefacts, the shimmer of light through interference. The darkness closed in like a screen going black, like all the systems of his life powering down for the final time.

Edward screamed, a sound like a hard drive failing, like all the data of a life being wiped clean.

And with that scream, he jolted awake in his bed. Morning light streamed through the smart windows, which had automatically adjusted to wake him gently. The city outside hummed with the sounds of life resuming, buses running their routes, shop shutters rising, people calling greetings to one another in voices unfiltered by digital compression.

His fitness tracker vibrated gently, registering that he was awake and beginning the day's health monitoring routines.

He was alive. The system was still running.

CHAPTER FIVE:
Christmas Day

Edward woke with the sun streaming through his smart windows, which had automatically adjusted their tint to optimise his circadian rhythm. For the first time in years, he didn't curse the brightness or reach immediately for his phone to check overnight market movements. Instead, he sat bolt upright, sheets tangled around him like network cables, chest heaving as if he'd been running a marathon through cyberspace.

"I'm alive," he whispered, his voice hoarse but real. His hand pressed to his chest, half-expecting to find emptiness where his heart should be, but there it was: the steady, analogue beat of biological life. No app could replicate that rhythm, no algorithm could optimise that essential human subroutine. "I'm alive. The system is still running."

He leaped from bed like a man whose entire operating system had been upgraded overnight, laughed out loud, a rusty sound, startling even to himself, like audio hardware being tested after years of disuse. He tried again, louder, until laughter echoed through the cold apartment, a virus of joy infecting every corner of his sterile environment.

The chains were gone. The grave was closed. The boy's crutch was only a nightmare, a prediction that could still be prevented.

Christmas morning was here, and for the first time in decades, Edward Sloane was ready for an upgrade, to install a new version of himself.

*

A Changed Man

He threw on jeans and a T-shirt, not the carefully coordinated business casual his image consultant had selected, but whatever came to hand first. His hair was uncombed, his face unshaven, and he felt more authentic than he had in years. He rushed to the balcony, the smart glass retracting automatically as it sensed his approach.

The Thames glittered in the pale sun like a stream of data flowing through the city. Families hurried along the pavements below, arms loaded with presents wrapped in paper rather than shipped in cardboard, children pulling parents toward shop windows that displayed wonders no algorithm had curated.

A boy trudged past on the street below, clutching a football that looked like it had been played with rather than just purchased.

"You there!" Edward called, his voice carrying strangely in the open air. He leaned over the rail, startled by the force of his own shout. "You, boy! What day is it?"

The child stopped, squinting upward into the winter sun. For a moment he could see nothing but mirrored glass and shadow, until Edward waved furiously.

"What day?" the boy shouted back, hand to his ear.

"It's Christmas Day, innit!" he added, grinning once he caught the question.

Edward clapped his hands together, the sound echoing off the building's facade. "Christmas Day! I haven't missed it! The system is still running!" He pulled out his wallet, removed a handful of crisp fifty-pound notes, not transferred digitally, but physical currency he could feel between his fingers. "Run to Ludgate Hill, to the butchers! Buy the biggest turkey they have, no, two! The best ones they've got! And keep the change for yourself!"

The boy's eyes widened as the notes fluttered down like confetti. He whooped, sprinting away with the kind of energy that no battery could store. Edward laughed until tears ran down his face, salt water that no device could replicate.

*

The Shopping Spree

Edward strode through the city streets, moving with purpose that had nothing to do with quarterly targets or productivity metrics. For the first time in years, he walked instead of driving, feeling the pavement beneath his feet, breathing air that hadn't been filtered through climate control systems.

He hit every shop that was open on Christmas morning, the corner newsagent run by a family who had known every customer's name for twenty years, the bakery where bread was made by hand rather than machine. Even a toy shop, improbably open, its window lights glowing against the grey day.

Inside, the owner, a widow with no children of her own, who kept the shutters up each Christmas morning in case some desperate parent had forgotten a gift, looked up in surprise as Edward entered. She helped him select toys not by what algorithms said children wanted, but by what she knew had brought joy for decades.

His arms filled with parcels wrapped in brown paper and tied with string, packaging that required human hands to open. Chocolates from a confectioner who still made truffles by hand. Board games that required no Wi-Fi connection. Jumpers knitted by people rather than machines. A cricket set for the Carter children. A stuffed reindeer for Toby, chosen not because it was trending but because its eyes reminded Edward of wonder itself.

By midday, a delivery van, one of the old-fashioned kinds driven by humans rather than GPS, pulled up outside the Carter flats, stacked to the roof with packages that bore Edward's handwriting rather than printed labels. He followed on foot, grinning like a child who had discovered that generosity was the ultimate app, one that ran on the human heart's operating system.

*

The Carters' Gift

Ben Carter opened the door wearing a Christmas jumper that had clearly been knitted by a relative with more love than skill. His face showed the weariness of a man trying to make Christmas special on a budget that allowed for little magic. When he saw Edward standing there surrounded by packages, his expression shifted through confusion, surprise, and finally something approaching hope.

"Mr... Mr Sloane?"

"Merry Christmas, Ben!" Edward cried, bustling into the flat like Santa updated for the digital age but running on analogue kindness. He dropped parcels on the table until toys and ribbons tumbled everywhere like data overflow from a generous server. "For the children. For your wife. And where's the boy? Where's Toby?"

Toby peeked out from under a blanket on the sofa, paper crown crooked on his head like a user interface element that refused to align properly. His cough was still there, a persistent error in his system that needed debugging, but his eyes were bright as LED displays.

Edward knelt to the boy's level, handling the stuffed reindeer like precious hardware. "From Father Christmas," he said solemnly, meeting Toby's eyes directly rather than looking through him as he had for so long. "He asked me to deliver this personally."

"Thank you, sir," Toby whispered, hugging the reindeer with the fierce love that children reserve for things that exist purely to be loved.

Edward's throat closed like a program hitting an exception handler. He turned to Ben, his voice thick with emotion that had been compressed for too long. "We'll get Toby proper care, private doctors, specialists, whatever it takes to fix this bug in his system. I have instructed a doctor to be here within the hour and to provide medication, today. You've been carrying too much load on insufficient resources."

Ben's mouth opened and closed like a computer trying to process unexpected input. His wife pressed a hand to her lips, tears brimming like overflowing data buffers, emotions too large for the limited storage of her heart.

"Sir, I... we can't possibly..." Ben began, but Edward held up a hand.

"You can, and you will. Consider it a system upgrade long overdue." Edward's voice grew serious, the CEO returning but tempered now with humanity. "Ben, I've been running faulty code for years. Treating people like depreciated assets instead of... instead of the most valuable part of any system." He looked around the small flat, seeing not cramped quarters but a home rich with the kind of wealth that couldn't be measured in cryptocurrency. "This family, this love, you've been running premium software on basic hardware, and I never gave you the resources you deserved."

"Merry Christmas," Edward said softly, and for once, he meant every syllable like a prayer uploaded directly to whatever server managed human souls.

*

Dinner

Later, Edward climbed the steps to Freddie's flat in Camden, clutching a bottle of champagne that cost more than most people's weekly groceries but was worth less than the chance to reconnect with family. The building was old, pre-digital in its character, with stairs that creaked like dial-up internet sounds and walls that told stories no algorithm could analyse.

He hesitated outside the door, nerves prickling like static electricity. His social skills felt rusty, like software that hadn't been updated in years. He had refused this invitation so many times through carefully crafted text messages and emails that cited "prior commitments" and "unavoidable obligations" excuses that were technically true but emotionally false.

But he knocked.

The door flew open, music and warmth spilling out like data from an overflowing server. Freddie, in his Santa hat that had clearly survived multiple Christmas seasons, gaped at his uncle as if he were witnessing a software miracle.

"Uncle Ed? Is this real or am I looking at a deepfake?"

Edward held up the champagne bottle, feeling awkward as a user trying to navigate an unfamiliar interface. "I hear there's a seat at your table. I know I should have RSVP'd earlier, but…"

For a heartbeat, Freddie stared, processing this unexpected input, then whooped so loud the neighbours leaned out of windows like pop-up notifications.

He hugged Edward so hard the man wheezed; the embrace carrying years of accumulated hope and forgiveness.

"I knew it! I knew you'd come one year! Mum's going to cry, happy tears, obviously. She kept saying you just needed the right algorithm to find your way back to us."

"Mum!" Freddie yelled into the kitchen. "Look who finally showed up!"
Hannah appeared, wiping her hands on a tea towel, eyes already brimming. For a second she looked ten years younger, as if Edward's arrival had rewound time itself. "Edward," she whispered, then hugged him with the quiet ferocity only a sister could muster.

Inside, the flat buzzed with the beautiful chaos of human connection unmediated by screens. Laughter mixed with conversation, glasses clinked with precision, and roast goose filled the air with smells that no delivery app could replicate. Someone shoved a Christmas cracker into Edward's hand; Freddie yanked it with the enthusiasm of a child, and a paper crown tumbled onto Edward's head like a user permission upgrade.

For the first time in decades, he laughed without calculating the energy expenditure, spoke without measuring the ROI of his words. He looked around at Freddie's friends, strangers who smiled as if he belonged in their network, young people who asked about his work not to network but because they were genuinely curious about the human behind the corporate profile.

"You know," said a girl with purple hair and a vintage band T-shirt, "Freddie talks about you all the time. Says you're brilliant but just forgot how to be happy."

Edward felt something warm spread through his chest like a successful software patch. Wealth, he thought, had never looked like this, not the digital numbers in his portfolio, but the analogue richness of human connection, the compound interest of love freely given.

*

Back at the Office

The next morning, the glass tower of Sloane & Marks LLP powered up earlier than usual, its systems running with renewed purpose. Edward sat in the boardroom, but instead of scowling at spreadsheets, he was grinning at his phone, not at stock prices or email notifications, but at photos from Freddie's party that someone had sent him via a group chat he'd been added to.

At nine o'clock, Ben Carter arrived, expecting another day of digital drudgery. He carried a reusable coffee cup that had seen better days and wore the same tired expression that had become his default setting. He froze at the sight of his boss holding a paper cup of hot chocolate, not optimised for caffeine efficiency, but chosen for comfort.

"Morning, Ben," Edward said warmly, gesturing to a chair. "Merry Christmas. How's Toby feeling?"

Ben blinked, processing this unexpected kindness like a computer receiving a software update. "Sir? He's... he's better, thank you. The medication you arranged, it's already helping."

"Good. Excellent." Edward leaned forward, his body language open rather than defensive. "Ben, I've been running some analysis, on myself, actually. Turns out I've been a terrible manager. Optimising for all the wrong variables."

He slid a document across the table, not a termination notice or performance review, but a promotion letter with salary figures that made Ben's eyes widen.

"Senior partner. Four times your current salary, full health coverage for the family, and flexible working arrangements. You can work from home when Toby needs you. Real flexibility, not the fake kind where I passive-aggressively punish you for having human needs."

Ben's eyes filled with tears that he tried to blink away, his hands shaking as he read the document. "Sir, I don't know what to say."

"Say you'll help me rewrite how this company operates. Less like a machine, more like... well, like humans working together toward something meaningful."

*

Acts of Kindness

Edward didn't stop there. The change in his programming seemed to cascade through every aspect of his life, like a system-wide update that touched every application.

He tipped 100% at the coffee shop where he'd been buying the same order for five years without ever learning the barista's name. (It was Jessica, and she had a toddler and dreams of opening her own café.) He donated so generously to the homeless shelter that volunteers hugged him in disbelief, tears mixing with the joy of people who'd forgotten that some humans still ran on generosity.exe.

At the children's hospital, he didn't just write a cheque; he served soup himself, laughing when a six-year-old asked if he was Santa's accountant. "Something like that," he replied, realising that Christmas magic was just another word for humans choosing to be kind when they didn't have to be.

He set up a fund for the paediatric ward that would provide not just equipment but experiences, art therapy, music programs, visits from therapy dogs. Things that couldn't be quantified in medical metrics but that made the healing process more human.

He paid off mortgages for staff who were drowning in debt, not as tax write-offs but as investments in human dignity. He listened, really listened, when people spoke, putting away his phone and making eye contact like a person rather than a network node.

And everywhere he went, Edward Sloane felt lighter, as if each act of kindness deleted another file from the malware of miserliness that had infected his soul.

*

Reputation Renewed

Word spread through the financial district with the speed of viral content. "Sloane? Buying toys for kids? Paying off a colleague's mortgage? What's his angle?" The City didn't know what to make of it, its algorithms struggling to process this unexpected behavioural change.

Some called it a breakdown, others, a publicity stunt. Social media buzzed with theories: mid-life crisis, tax avoidance scheme, early signs of dementia. The human tendency to assume ulterior motives was strong, especially in a world where genuine kindness had become so rare it seemed suspicious.

But those who knew him, Freddie, Ben, Toby, saw the truth. Edward had debugged his life, patched out the errors that had made him treat humans like legacy code to be optimised away.

His business grew, but differently now. Profits came not from exploitation but from innovation that served human needs. His reputation transformed from feared to respected, from efficient to effective. Not because he'd become soft, but because he'd learned that the most sophisticated algorithm was still useless without the human heart to give it direction.

*

Five Years Later

Five years on, Edward stood once more in the Carter home, now a larger house with a garden where children played analogue games that required no batteries. The Christmas tree brushed the ceiling, decorated with ornaments made by hand rather than purchased online, each one carrying a story, a memory, a moment of human connection.

Toby, taller now and healthier, dashed between cousins with the energy of a child whose system had been successfully debugged and optimised for joy rather than just survival. His laughter was a sound Edward had learned to value above any notification alert.

Edward sat in a comfortable armchair, not a designer piece but something chosen for how it felt rather than how it looked, nursing a mug of mulled wine that someone had made by following their grandmother's recipe rather than a YouTube tutorial. Around him, the Carter family's extended network had gathered: Ben explaining board game rules to children who listened with the patience of those who knew love was the most important rule; Ben's wife directing kitchen operations with the efficiency of someone who had learned to manage abundance rather than scarcity.

This, Edward thought, was true wealth not the number in his portfolio, but the laughter in this room, the trust in these relationships, the knowledge that he had helped write the code for this happiness.

Freddie appeared beside his chair, grinning and slightly drunk on Christmas cheer and actual alcohol. "You know, Uncle Ed, five years ago I would never have believed this."

"What?"

"You. Here. Actually enjoying yourself instead of calculating the opportunity cost of not working."

Edward chuckled, setting down his mug. "I learned something important, Freddie. All those years I spent optimising for efficiency, I was solving the wrong problem entirely."

"Which was?"

"I thought the goal was to accumulate resources. Turns out the goal is to use them well."

*

The New Christmas Morning

The following year, older now and with hair more silver than brown, Edward walked with Toby across a frost-covered bridge over the Thames. The city stretched out before them, its lights beginning to twinkle as evening approached, but Edward no longer saw it as a marketplace to be exploited. He saw it as a network of human stories, each light representing a life, a family, a possibility for connection.

"Uncle Ed," Toby said, his voice carrying the confidence of a child who had learned that the adults in his life could be trusted to stick around, "why do you always get so quiet on Christmas morning?"

Edward paused, watching a family of tourists take selfies with Tower Bridge in the background, their faces glowing not just from their phone screens but from genuine happiness. "Because I'm running a memory diagnostic," he said, then laughed at his own technological metaphor. "I'm remembering, Toby. Remembering how close I came to missing all of this. How close I came to crashing entirely."

"Not crashing," Toby said firmly, with the certainty of someone who had faced his own system failures and come through stronger. "You just needed a reboot. You changed the code. That's not crashing. That's upgrading."

Edward felt his chest swell with something that no financial app could measure but that was worth more than all his accumulated wealth. The boy was right, of course. He hadn't broken down; he had broken through.

They walked on, their footsteps echoing off the bridge's Victorian stonework, two generations connected not by blood but by the kind of love that chose to persist despite bugs and glitches and system failures.

*

The Full Circle

Years later, when Edward's hair had gone completely white and his step had slowed (though his heart had never been stronger), he found himself once again in his glass apartment on Christmas Eve. But this time, he wasn't alone.

Ben Carter sat across from him, now a full partner in the company they had built together, one that prioritised human welfare alongside profit margins. Freddie was there too, with his partner and their adopted daughter, all of them taking turns reading "A Christmas Carol" aloud because it had become their tradition.

Toby, now a teenager with dreams of becoming a doctor himself, looked up from his tablet. He was coding, but for fun, creating apps that helped other kids with chronic illnesses connect and support each other.

"Uncle Ed," he said, "do you ever wonder what would have happened if you hadn't changed? If you'd kept running the old program?"

Edward considered this, looking around at the warmth that filled his apartment, not the artificial warmth of climate control, but the human warmth of people who chose to spend their time together. "I try not to think about it too much," he said. "That version of me was deprecated for good reason."

"But sometimes?"

"Sometimes I think about a very lonely man who forgot that the most sophisticated technology in the world is still just a tool. And tools are only as valuable as the purposes they serve."

Hannah appeared from the kitchen, carrying a tray of tea and the kind of homemade biscuits that required time and attention, resources Edward had once considered too expensive to spend. "Are you getting philosophical again?" she asked, kissing the top of his head. "You know that's a Christmas tradition now."

"Everything's a Christmas tradition now," Edward replied, grinning. "I have years of missed celebrations to catch up on."

Outside, snow began to fall, each flake unique as a handwritten line of code, beautiful and temporary and perfect in its inefficiency.

*

Closing Note

And from that day to the last of his life, Edward Sloane kept Christmas in his heart every day of the year, not as a scheduled event in his calendar app, but as a constant background process running on the operating system of human kindness.

He became as good a friend, as good an uncle, and as good a man as London had ever known. His company flourished not because it extracted maximum value from human resources, but because it invested in human potential. His algorithms served people rather than enslaving them. His technology connected rather than isolated.

His employees no longer worked in fear but with purpose, their creativity unleashed rather than constrained. The office became warmer, literally and figuratively, a place where people brought their whole selves rather than just their productive output.

To those who saw him, it was always said that he truly knew how to keep Christmas well, not just the holiday, but the spirit of generosity and connection that the season represented. He had learned to see humans not as users to be optimised, but as individuals to be celebrated.

If any man alive possessed that knowledge, the understanding that the most advanced technology would always be the human heart, surely it was he.

His transformation became a case study taught in business schools, not for its profit margins but for its proof that companies could succeed by serving human flourishing rather than just shareholder value. Young entrepreneurs would reference "The Sloane Protocol" - the practice of measuring success not just in financial returns but in human welfare.

And so, as the Carters liked to remind him each year with a toast that never failed to bring tears to his eyes, as they raised their glasses in the warm glow of a Christmas tree that had been chosen for its beauty rather than its efficiency:

"To debugging the human heart and may we all learn to run on the operating system of love."

"God bless us, Every One," they would add, the words carrying across the years like the most important data transmission ever sent, a message of hope that no algorithm could corrupt, no virus could delete, and no system failure could erase.

In a world increasingly run by machines, Edward Sloane had learned the most important lesson of all: the most powerful program ever written was human kindness, and it was open source, available to all, and improved with every act of sharing.

The ghost of his old self, the one who had measured everything and valued nothing, had been successfully uninstalled. In its place ran something far more sophisticated: a human being who understood that love was not a bug in the system, but its most essential feature.

sys.exit(0)

or

The End

Printed in Dunstable, United Kingdom